January

February

March

April

May

June

July

August

September

October

November

December

Please Try to Remember the **FIRST** of **OCTEMBER!**

OCTEMBER

By **Dr. Seuss**
writing as
Theo. LeSieg
illustrated by Art Cummings

HarperCollins *Children's Books*

Essex County
Council Libraries

Trademark of Random House Inc. William Collins Sons & Co Ltd, Authorised User

15 17 19 20 18 16 14

ISBN-13: 978-0-00-171316-1
ISBN-10: 0-00-171316-7 (paperback)
ISBN-10: 0-00-171169-5 (hardback)

© 1977 by Dr. Seuss and A. S. Geisel
Illustrations © 1977 by Random House Inc.
A Beginner Book published by arrangement with
Random House Inc., New York, USA
First published in Great Britain 1978

Printed and bound in Hong Kong

Everyone wants
a big green kangaroo.

Maybe, perhaps,
you would like
to have TWO.

I want you to have them.
I'll buy them for you . . .

. . . if you'll wait

till the First of Octember.

Everyone wants
a new skateboard TV.
Some people want two.
And some people want three.

Perhaps you want four?

Well, that's O.K. with me . . .

. . . if you'll wait

till the First of Octember.

Just say what you want.

You want pickles on trees?

Want to swing
through the air
on a flying trapeze?

Just say what you want,
and whatever you say,
you'll get
on Octember the First.

WHAT A DAY!

When October comes round,
you can play a hot tune
on your very expensive
new Jook-a-ma-Zoon!

I wish you could play it

in May or in June.

But May is too early.

And June is too soon.

When October gets here,
no work! And no school!

We'll build you a playhouse!
We'll build you a pool!
We would build them
right now,
but right now
is too cool.

And we'll buy you
a wonderful
Jeep-a-Fly kite!

We will!
If you'll wait
till the month is just right.

Octember's the best
because March is too dusty.
And April won't do
because April's too gusty.

What <u>more</u> do you want?

Do you and your dog
want more time to relax? . . .
Less time on your feet
and more time on your backs? . . .
More time in the air
and less time on the ground? . . .

You'll get it
as soon as
October comes round.

Want to take a great trip?
Well, I know a great ship!

It sails
to Alaska,
Nebraska and Sweden,
making stops
in Ga-Dopps
and the Garden of Eden.

And it sails on the First of October!

What <u>else</u> do you want?

Want to play a new sport?

In October
we'll build you
a Hock-Zocker court!

You'll get all that you want.
You just write out your list.
<u>Everyone</u> has an October First list.

Write slowly now!
Don't break your wrist.

Then one of these days
the October First van
will drive up to your house
just as fast as it can.

Whatever you want,
you will get in big bags,
and boxes and crates
with your name on the tags.

You'll have
rockets to shoot.

You'll have fireworks
that burst . . .

. . . on the wonderful

night of

OCTEMBER
THE
FIRST!

On the First of Octember
you'll stay up all night,
drinking 66 six-packs
of Doodle Delight.

Whatever
you ask for,
I want
you to get.

But October—
I'm sorry—
just isn't <u>here</u> yet.

SO . . .

Be sure

to be here.

Be sure you're in town

on October the First . . .

. . . when
the
money
comes
down!

It doesn't
come down much
in March
or November—
or even September . . .

. . . or in August,

October,

July

or December.

But
EVERYTHING'S
YOURS . . .

. . . on the First
of Octember!

On the First
of Octember?

Thank <u>you</u>!
I'll remember.

Learning to read is fun with Beginner Books

I CAN READ IT ALL BY MYSELF

Beginner Books

FIRST get started with:

Ten Apples Up On Top
Dr. Seuss

Go Dog Go
P D Eastman

Put Me in the Zoo
Robert LopShire

THEN gain confidence with:

Dr. Seuss's ABC*
Dr. Seuss

Fox in Sox*
Dr. Seuss

Green Eggs and Ham*
Dr. Seuss

Hop on Pop*
Dr. Seuss

I Can Read With My Eyes Shut
Dr. Seuss

I Wish That I Had Duck Feet
Dr. Seuss

One Fish, Two Fish*
Dr. Seuss

Oh, the Thinks You Can Think!
Dr. Seuss

Please Try to Remember the First of Octember
Dr. Seuss

Wacky Wednesday
Dr. Seuss

Are You My Mother?
P D Eastman

Because a Little Bug Went Ka-choo!
Rosetta Stone

Best Nest
P D Eastman

Come Over to My House
Theo. LeSieg

The Digging-est Dog
Al Perkins

I Am Not Going to Get Up Today!
Theo. LeSieg

It's Not Easy Being a Bunny!
Marilyn Sadler

I Want to Be Somebody New
Robert LopShire

Maybe You Should Fly a Jet!
Theo. LeSieg

Robert the Rose Horse
Joan Heilbroner

The Very Bad Bunny
Joan Heilbroner

THEN take off with:

The Cat in the Hat*
Dr. Seuss

The Cat in the Hat Comes Back*
Dr. Seuss

Oh Say Can You Say?
Dr. Seuss

My Book About Me
Dr. Seuss

A Big Ball of String
Marion Holland

Chitty Chitty Bang Bang!
Ian Fleming

A Fish Out of Water
Helen Palmer

A Fly Went By
Mike McClintock

The King, the Mice and the Cheese
N & E Gurney

Sam and the Firefly
P D Eastman

BERENSTAIN BEAR BOOKS
By Stan & Jan Berenstain

The Bear Detectives

The Bear Scouts

The Bears' Christmas

The Bears' Holiday

The Bears' Picnic

The Berenstain Bears and the Missing Dinosaur Bones

The Big Honey Hunt

The Bike Lesson

THEN you won't quite be ready to go to college. But you'll be well on your way!

*From the Dr. Seuss Classic Collection